CURSED

CURSED

SINKHOLE

CURSED

SUSAN KOEHLER

DARBY CREEK

MINNEAPOLIS

Darby Creek
An imprint of Lerner Publishing Group, Inc.
241 First Avenue North
Minneapolis, MN 55401 USA

For reading levels and more information, look up this title at www.lernerbooks.com.

Cover and interior images: Serafima82/Shutterstock (watch); Alena Ohneva/Shutterstock (smoke background); Copyright © 2020 KADIVAR07/Shutterstock (background); Milano M/Shutterstock (chapter number background)

Main body text set in Janson Text LT Std.
Typeface provided by Adobe Systems.

Library of Congress Cataloging-in-Publication Data

Names: Koehler, Susan, 1963– author.
Title: Cursed / Susan Koehler.
Description: Minneapolis : Darby Creek, [2023] | Series: Sinkhole | Audience: Ages 11–18. | Audience: Grades 7–9. | Summary: Eli Hancock's luck seems to improve after he finds a gold coin on undeveloped property, and when he later finds a pocket watch in the same place, strange things start to happen, making Eli wonder if he is instead cursed.
Identifiers: LCCN 2022024053 (print) | LCCN 2022024054 (ebook) | ISBN 9781728475509 (lib. bdg.) | ISBN 9781728477978 (pbk.) | ISBN 9781728479521 (eb pdf)
Subjects: CYAC: Luck—Fiction. | Popularity—Fiction. | High schools—Fiction. | Schools—Fiction. | LCGFT: High interest-low vocabulary books. | Novels.
Classification: LCC PZ7.1.K6732 Cu 2023 (print) | LCC PZ7.1.K6732 (ebook) | DDC [Fic]—dc23

LC record available at https://lccn.loc.gov/2022024053
LC ebook record available at https://lccn.loc.gov/2022024054

Manufactured in the United States of America
1 – TR – 12/15/22

Dude, it's not supernatural. It's science." Eli
Hancock balances a stack of books in the
cradle of his left arm and uses his right hand to
secure the combination lock.

"I'm just saying, one day the ground is
solid, and the next thing you know, *whoosh*!"
Freddy Santana slams his locker closed for
dramatic effect. "The desert opens up and
swallows bushes and rocks and probably some
little lizards and stuff like that."

Eli laughs as he waits for Freddy to replace
his lock. "But you're forgetting the fact that

for years that desert was punctured by oil wells. Those sinkholes in Wink County can be explained."

"Yeah," Freddy interrupts. "My mom can explain it. She says it's the wrath of angry spirits."

"As I was about to say," Eli continues, "the rock beneath the soil is really unstable because of all the drilling for oil and gas that's been done around here. I mean, this whole area is like a giant pincushion. Have you watched the local news? Some geologists say that in about ten years—"

He's interrupted again. This time by Nolan Bridwell, who knocks the books from Eli's hands, the same way he's done a hundred times before. "Sorry, dweeb!" Nolan and his posse erupt in laughter. "I wasn't watching where I was going!"

They swagger off down the hallway, and as Eli kneels on the floor, retrieving his books, he hears Nolan's mocking tone, high-pitched and nasal. "Texas is like a giant pincushion." More laughter follows.

Adjusting his glasses and trying to regain his composure, Eli says, "I hate that guy."

"Hate is a strong word, my friend." Freddy extends a hand to pull Eli up from the dirty tile floor. "Just ignore him. Consider it a compliment. There are worse things he could call you."

"Yeah," Eli concedes, "but he's got a really small vocabulary."

The two friends laugh and walk side by side. Freddy says, "You know, if you actually carried your books in your backpack, this might not happen."

"My backpack is reserved for notebooks, supplies, lunch, and snacks. I have a system," Eli reminds him. "And look at me. Even if the books fit, they'd probably pull me over. I'd land on my back and flail around like a turtle on its shell. Imagine what Nolan could do with that."

"True," Freddy says, and he laughs at the image. "Maybe you should just scale back on the super-intense classes, man. Do your back a favor."

Eli and Freddy exit Foggy Creek High School, blinded momentarily by a blast of bright sunlight. Once their eyes adjust, they both focus on Nolan Bridwell's squad ambling down the middle of the road. No doubt looking for trouble.

"How about we implement Plan B and take the long way home?" Eli asks. "I don't want to run into him again."

"Sure thing," Freddy says. They turn from the main road and walk toward the scrubby terrain, heading for what was once a thriving cattle ranch called the Broken Brand. Now it's just a series of abandoned fields. Sporadic fence posts line the property, but there's no fence anymore. A faded "No Trespassing" sign stands just off the road, but it's leaning slightly to the right and easy to ignore.

As they reach the edge of the desolate property, they stop. A new sign towers above the old, familiar one. "Future Home of Foggy Creek Estates," Freddy reads. They stand in its shadow, perplexed. "What the heck is this?"

Eli adjusts his books and his glasses. "According to the sign, it'll be a mixed-use development. Single-family homes, a movie theater, a retail center . . ."

"Yeah, I can read that," Freddy says. "But how can they do this?"

"Again, according to the sign," Eli says, "it's the work of developer Kit Landau. I guess he bought the property."

"Man, nobody even told me it was for sale," Freddy quips. "It still looks like a bunch of dry grass to me. And it's also still the best way to avoid Bridwell's brigade. I say we cross as usual."

Eli shrugs. "I guess until they start actually building, nobody will care." The two friends walk past the faded "No Trespassing" sign and onto the Broken Brand.

Wandering in their own wilderness, they talk freely. About video games. About pizza. About sci-fi books and comics. About anything but Nolan. About anything that makes them feel connected, and alive, and in lockstep with one another.

Until suddenly, in one fateful step, the Earth gives way, and Freddy is pulled waist-deep into churning, sinking mud.

2

Eli throws his books aside and reaches for Freddy with both hands. Heat radiates from his face and his glasses fog, but he feels Freddy's tight grip on his arm. Planting his feet firmly on the ground and summoning all his strength, Eli is able to lift Freddy from the thick mud.

Hearts pounding, gasping for breath, both boys crab crawl until they feel a safe distance from the hole. Finally, Freddy speaks. "Dude, the ground just opened up underneath me. Do you think there are angry spirits here?"

Eli sighs. "No, I think there was a hole in the ground, and you weren't watching where you were going."

"Where are your books?" Freddy asks. "Did they get sucked into the Earth?"

Eli laughs. "No, I threw them over there." He points to his side and adds, "On perfectly dry ground."

Freddy nods at Eli, calming enough to smile. He turns to brush away mud from the bottom of his backpack. "Good thing my books all fit in here. See, if I had all super-intense classes, I'd probably owe the school for textbooks that got sucked into the Earth."

But Eli is barely listening. After cleaning his foggy, mud-splattered lenses with his t-shirt, he adjusts his glasses and spots something shiny and gold perched on the edge of the muddy hole. "Hey, look," he says, crawling toward the curious object.

"Don't get too close!" Freddy warns.

But now Eli is not listening at all. He is crawling toward the shiny object, stretching his arm out to reach for it. He pulls it from the mud and realizes it's a coin. He wipes away the mud and says, "1890."

Freddy's forehead wrinkles. "There's a coin worth $18.90?"

"No," Eli says, "I'm sure this coin is worth a lot more than that. It was minted in 1890. So it must be pure gold." He stands and tucks the coin into the pocket of his jeans. "And you know what they say. Finders keepers."

Freddy stands and says, "Hey, maybe you should leave it here. Maybe it belongs to the angry spirits. You don't want to get on their bad side. I think I'd rather face Nolan Bridwell than the wrath of angry spirits."

"We should hang out here for a while," Eli suggests. "Do a little exploring. Maybe there are more old coins or artifacts or—"

"Are you kidding, dude?!" Freddy looks around nervously. "Can we get out of here? This whole quicksand thing has made me a little freaked out. Actually, make that a LOT freaked out!"

Eli collects his books. Conscious of Freddy's mud-covered jeans and shoes, he says,

"Do you want to come to my house and use the washing machine? My dad is picking up groceries after work. You could probably even stay for dinner."

Freddy sighs. "Thanks. But I have to be home when my little sister gets off the bus. Mom's working the late shift at the diner today." He looks down at his pants and sighs again. "I'm gonna have to bribe the little blabbermouth with candy so she doesn't say anything to my mom. How would I ever be able to explain this?"

"Why not just tell the truth?" Eli asks.

With a mix of shock and fear, Freddy says, "Are you kidding?! If my mom finds out we trespassed, she'll flip. And don't even get me started on the angry spirits!"

The two boys turn to continue their journey across the Broken Brand but stop suddenly. They look at each other, then back at the ground. Where only moments before, Freddy had been sucked into a muddy hole, now there is nothing unusual. There is grass. There is dirt. But no mud. And no hole.

"H-how could that happen?" Freddy stammers. "Y-you were here. You saw it."

"Interesting phenomenon," Eli mumbles. "Perhaps we've found the potential site of a new sinkhole. Somehow, the ground was able to right itself. Maybe we should take soil samples and–"

"Maybe we should get out of here!" Freddy says, and he begins walking with heavy, purposeful steps. Eli shrugs and follows, multiple hypotheses swarming in his head.

As they continue across the hot, dry field, the mud on Freddy's pants begins to dry. It falls in broken cakes with every step. They reach the road that borders the west end of the Broken Brand and part ways. Freddy heads toward his sister's bus stop, stomping his feet, forcing dried cakes of mud to fall from his shoes and jeans. Eli looks back and smiles as his friend marches away.

Once at home, Eli pushes the events of the afternoon aside. He dives into homework and only comes up for air once he's checked the first two items off his to-do list. He organizes his stacks of materials. The textbooks and notebooks he's finished with move to the bottom. Materials for the next items on the list move to the top. Hovering in the middle are the items for the "if I have time" task list. Time for a break.

Eli stands and stretches. He remembers the coin and pulls it from his pocket. It feels warm in his hand as he studies the markings once more. Etched on the front, a woman's head is adorned with a crown that says "Liberty." All around her, stars line the coin, and beneath her, the year 1890 glimmers in the fluorescent light of Eli's bedroom. "Nearly mint condition. Gotta be worth a bundle," he mumbles to himself, and then he places the coin on the nightstand by his bed.

Eli sits back down at the desk and opens his laptop, eager to find the coin's value. But before he can begin his search, the front door opens and he hears his dad's voice calling, "Eli! A little help with the groceries, please!"

Eli closes the laptop and jumps up from his chair. When he reaches the doorway, he turns back once more to look at the coin. He blinks twice and adjusts his glasses. Because as crazy and impossible as it sounds, the coin seems to be glowing.

Eli and his dad sit on the living room sofa and
eat Italian subs from the grocery's deli. Side
by side, they chew and nod and watch the local
news. The deli subs are their grocery-night
ritual. Eating in front of the local news is their
every-night ritual.

There's a story about Kit Landau and the
new development planned for the old Broken
Brand. They show a photo of the sign, and
then a 3-D digital model of the mixed-use
development. Sketches show single-family
homes, a movie theater, and a retail center.

"Totally irresponsible." Eli's dad scoffs and shakes his head. "Another example of the county disregarding advice from its own Department of Environmental Management. I don't know why they pay us if they're just going to ignore us."

Eli starts to say something, but he's just taken a bite. And by the time he chews and swallows, the news has moved on to wildfires, a car accident, a political scandal, and lastly, a human-interest story about a lost dog that finally made it home to the family that never gave up hope.

By the time they're cleaning up their few dishes, the conversation has moved away from the local news. Eli's dad asks, "So, any word on the science fair project? When will they let you know?"

Eli shrugs. "Should be soon. Trying not to think about it. Don't want to get my hopes up, just in case . . ."

His dad nods and says, "Understandable. But you should feel confident. I think you've got a good chance of going to State. People don't realize how much influence barometric pressure has over their moods, their perception of pain, their behavior—"

His dad continues talking, but Eli is lost in thought. His entire project is built on the idea that changes in weather cause changes in people's behavior. His hypothesis relies on the idea that moods and behavior are largely a result of high or low air pressure.

But then, what about Nolan Bridwell? His irritating behavior is irritatingly consistent, rain or shine. It doesn't seem to be affected by rising or falling air pressure, which makes it even more irritating because it doesn't fit with Eli's hypothesis. And the personal anxiety Eli feels when Nolan approaches isn't a product of air pressure either. It's a side effect of Nolan. It's like the guy creates his own barometric pressure.

Eli shakes his head. He doesn't want to think about this. It's not consistent with his hypothesis. So, he says, "This hot, dry spell will continue all week. That's not good news for the fires." Then they veer off in a new direction. They talk about wildfires and political scandals and deli sandwiches and the little lost dog.

Eli all but forgets about the gold coin. He also forgets to tell his dad about crossing the Broken Brand, and about the hole and the mud and Freddy. Or maybe he doesn't forget. Maybe he decides to remain silent. Because maybe some things are better left unsaid.

They recede into their own worlds, Eli into homework and his dad into a book. Night folds itself upon them quietly until it's time to mark the end of another day.

Eli's dad stops at the bedroom door and leans his head in. "I'm off to bed," he says. "Don't stay up too late."

Eli closes his notebook and says, "Sounds like a plan. Good night." His eyelids are heavy, and his mind longs for rest. He doesn't put his things away and doesn't get his usual bedside glass of water. He just turns out the light and crawls under the covers.

Sleep comes easily to Eli. But that sleep is anything but restful. It's filled with strange, active dreams that seem so real. There's a train traveling through the western wilderness. A long, black steam engine.

In this dream, Eli hears the rattling rhythm of the train's wheels against the steel track. He feels the constant vibration as the wheels churn the air and move the heavy mammoth forward. He can smell the burning coal that produces the heat that produces the steam. And in his dream, he's there.

Only, Eli isn't traveling inside this train. It's as if he's clinging to the window and looking in as the train moves. Through the glass, he sees a young man's profile. This young man sits alone. Sandy hair covers his head and rests loosely on his neck and forehead.

The young man's clothes are neat, but they're well-worn and a little faded. His black pants and dusty boots could fit in many time periods, but the white shirt, gray vest, and long, dark jacket is definitely from another century. He holds a newspaper in his left hand and an old-style fountain pen in his right. After circling something in the newspaper, he lays it in the seat to his left. The young man's body obstructs the newspaper, but it's too far away for Eli to read anyway.

The young man seems nervous, Eli thinks from the window. The man's hand taps restlessly on his leg, his icy blue eyes dart about. Then he makes a sudden move. His right hand reaches beneath the dark jacket, into a small pocket on the front of his vest. He pulls out a round, gold pocket watch inscribed with the letter W. The watch is attached to a gold chain that keeps it tethered to the young man's vest. He presses a button on the top, and the watch opens. He checks the time, closes the watch, and moves to return it to his pocket.

But before he completes the task, something happens. Something shocking and unexpected. The young man's head lifts suddenly, and his blue eyes widen with fright. Eli feels the fear, the trembling, as if it is his own. He tries to see what the young man sees, but it's impossible. Through this dream window, Eli can only see the young man's profile and the watch, still clutched in his hand.

Eli hears the rattle of the train. He feels the man's fear and horror.

Eli awakens with a start. The images are gone. The sound of the wheels against the track is fading and the smell of the coal recedes. But in the distance, very clearly, he hears the haunting whine of a train whistle screaming in the night.

Sweat drenches Eli's face and drips down his neck. He sits up. He takes a few deep breaths, tries to escape the dream and reclaim his place in the rational world. In his room. In his bed.

Eli reaches for the glass of water that usually sits on his nightstand but feels nothing there. He turns, suddenly remembering that he didn't get the water before going to bed. And then Eli stops breathing for just a moment. Because on the nightstand, in the dark of his room, the gold coin glows like a full moon in a starless sky.

It's morning, and sunlight streams through the window. Daylight offers a fresh perspective. Eli shakes his head as if he can loosen the memory of the dream, as if he can somehow discard it and escape that tremor deep inside.

He grabs his backpack and takes one last look around his room to make sure he hasn't forgotten anything. His eyes land on the coin. It sits innocently on his nightstand. Sunlight accents the luster of its gold, and Eli laughs at himself for thinking it actually glowed. There must be some phenomenon with light and gold and the age of the coin.

But he doesn't have the time or the desire to figure it out right now. He accepts that there must be a scientific explanation. Usually, he would feel compelled to research the phenomenon and solve this puzzle. But for some reason, he doesn't feel that way. For some reason, he just wants to get rid of the coin.

So, Eli picks it up. He looks once more at the year, 1890. He looks at the word "Liberty" and the woman's profile and the stars. Then he tucks the coin into his pocket. He knows what he must do. He must return it to the Broken Brand. *Sure, it's probably worth money. But it's not worth the trouble*, Eli reasons.

Satisfied with his plan, he adjusts his glasses, grabs his stack of books, and heads for the car. On the drive to school, his dad reminds him to be confident, to advocate for himself, and to ask about the science fair project. Eli says he will, even though he knows he probably won't.

As they pull up at the drop-off zone, his dad has one more reminder. "Text me when you get home. I have a meeting this afternoon that might run late. But I want to know you've made it home safely."

Eli nods and exits the car, backpack on, books in his hands, and coin in his pocket. He uses his hip to close the door and sets off for his locker. Before homeroom, he plans to tell Freddy that he wants to cross the Broken Brand again to return the coin. He thinks he might tell Freddy about the dream, but he's not sure.

However, he doesn't get the chance to talk to Freddy. His science teacher, Mrs. Mendez, intercepts him in the hallway. Reading glasses dangle from a chain around her neck. They bounce against her flowery dress as she practically runs toward him.

"Eli!" she shouts, panting from the exertion and trying to regain normal breathing. "I want to be the first to tell you. I don't want you to just hear it on the morning announcements. Walk with me!" She's practically giddy with excitement. "I'm so glad you're in my homeroom. This is just perfect."

Eli closes his locker. He raises his eyebrows and shrugs at Freddy, who has just arrived. He follows Mrs. Mendez to her classroom. She takes a deep breath and says, "Eli, your project is moving on to State!"

Eli smiles. He's aware of the weight of the books in his hands, but they seem lighter. He feels taller. He holds his head a little higher. "That's awesome," he says. He wants to text his dad, but his hands are full and Mrs. Mendez apparently has more to say.

"The committee was very impressed with the correlation you showed between barometric pressure and human behavior." As she's talking, other members of her homeroom class arrive. She ignores them and continues. "It's rare for someone your age to study human behavior. It's quite impressive, really."

Eli thanks her and moves to his seat at the back of the room. It's not his preferred place to sit in any classroom, but homeroom has alphabetical seating, and Hancock happens to land him in the very last seat on the second row. To add to the irony, alphabetical seating puts Nolan Bridwell up front.

Eli watches as Nolan swaggers to his seat. "Yo, Mendez!" Nolan shouts. He's not actually trying to get her attention. He just wants to be the center of attention and own the room. He looks around and nods, satisfied that he's claimed his territory.

"Good morning, Mr. Bridwell," Mrs. Mendez says through tight lips. "That will be enough."

And then the morning announcements begin. After the regular rituals and the schedule reminders, the big announcement is made. "Huge congratulations to our own Eli Hancock. His science fair project has won district honors. It will be moving on to State. Great job, Eli! Foggy Creek salutes you!"

Mrs. Mendez beams. Every head turns in unison. They look to the back at Eli and applaud. Some shout praises. *Way to go, Eli! Woohoo! Eli's the big dog!*

Eli's face is suddenly warm. He knows the

color is rushing to it. He's trying to play it cool, but he's also happy. This is good.

It's all too much for Nolan. He waits for the applause to die down so that everyone can hear him. Then he can regain the attention. He leans back in his chair and turns his head in Eli's direction. "Yeah! Way to go, dw—"

But before he can finish the insult, he loses his balance. The chair tips over and scoots out from under him. Nolan Bridwell ends up on the floor. Mrs. Mendez rushes to his side. But he's not physically hurt. It's his ego that's bruised.

There's a small sprinkling of chuckles. And then some giggles. Soon, the entire class erupts in uncontrollable laughter. Nolan picks up his chair and slides back into it. This time, it's his face that is red. Beet red. He's gotten everyone's attention, but this is never the kind of attention Nolan Bridwell wants.

The bell rings. People stand, still laughing. They pat Eli on the back. They head into the hallway and begin to spread the hilarious story about Nolan Bridwell going bottoms up in homeroom.

Eli smiles. It's a good feeling. And then he's suddenly aware of the coin in his pocket. He doesn't normally believe in luck of any kind. But if there is such a thing as good luck, maybe he has found it. And suddenly, he's conflicted. Part of him still wants to return it to the Broken Brand. But another part of him thinks maybe, just maybe, there is more luck to be found.

Eli stands in front of his locker, but it's hard
to even think about what books he'll need
for studying and homework. People keep
interrupting his concentration. But he doesn't
mind. It's all high fives and fist bumps, pats on
the back, and *My man, Eli Hancock!*

Freddy is there at his side, letting the
spotlight spill over onto him. He seems to
enjoy this turn of events that has brought about
a new dynamic at Foggy Creek High. His
friend Eli is suddenly popular. And the best
part of the whole thing is that Nolan Bridwell

is nowhere in sight. In a single day, he's gone from being the center of attention to being the center of a joke.

"Dude, you're famous!" Freddy says. Eli no longer blushes in response. He's had hours to overcome the embarrassment of the attention. Now he embraces it.

"What can I say?" He shrugs. "My luck seems to be changing."

"And Nolan!" Freddy doubles over in laughter. "I heard about the whole chair thing. Man, I wish I had been there to see him sprawled out on the floor like the snake that he is."

Eli smiles and closes his locker. "I have to admit, it was pretty awesome."

The two friends turn to make their exit from the hallway. Only a few students linger. A few teachers stand at their doors on duty. A few more times, they say *Congratulations, Mr. Hancock! and Proud of you, Eli!*

As Eli and Freddy transition from the dimly lit hallway to the bright sunshine, both boys stop. They squint until their eyes adjust.

"Hey, can we cut across the Broken Brand again today?" Eli says.

Freddy is dumbfounded. "What? Risk stepping into quicksand and being sucked into the Earth by angry spirits? No, thank you."

Eli laughs. "You know there is no such thing. And we'll watch where we're going this time. I'm just thinking—"

"Thinking crazy!" Freddy interrupts. "You don't have to worry about Nolan. As a matter of fact, running into him today might be kind of satisfying!"

"It's not that," Eli explains. "You know, that coin and all. I told you, it's probably worth a lot of money. Before Kit Landau turns the place into a concrete jungle, we should check it out. We'll keep our eyes on the ground so we can look for artifacts." He smiles. "And avoid quicksand."

Freddy sighs. "I can't believe I'm letting you talk me into this. Okay, just one more time."

Again, they walk toward the scrubby wilderness that was once a thriving cattle plantation. Eli considers telling Freddy about the strange dream. The train. The young man. Remembering the terror in his icy blue eyes sends a chill down Eli's spine. And then he realizes this is the last thing he needs to share with his superstitious friend. Instead, he settles for the train whistle. Something concrete.

"Last night," Eli says, "it was the craziest thing. I woke up to this stupid train whistle. What the heck? Since when did trains start running through Foggy Creek in the middle of the night?"

Freddy stops. He scrunches his eyes and forehead. "Trains haven't run through Foggy Creek for decades, dude." Then he laughs. "I think you were dreaming!" Freddy seems satisfied that the mystery has been explained. But for Eli, the mystery is beginning to grow.

"Yeah, maybe it was a dream. But it sounded real. And I was sitting up in my bed. My eyes were open. I'm pretty sure I was awake." Eli seems to be trying to convince himself.

"Right," Freddy says. "Just like I was awake that time I dreamed my little sister taught my dog to talk, and the two of them kept telling knock-knock jokes." He laughs. "Remember that?"

Eli laughs. Just to be polite. But he isn't in the mood for humor right now. He makes a mental note to do some research about trains in Foggy Creek. Maybe a new route has been established. It seems he would have heard about it on the local news, but . . .

"Or what about that time I dreamed I could fly! Remember that one?" Freddy has completely moved on to reliving his fantastical dreams.

"Isn't that the one where you went to the Grand Canyon? And you flew with a bald eagle?"

"Yeah," Freddy reminisces. "It was awesome!"

Eli laughs. "A bald eagle and a national landmark? You have very patriotic dreams, my friend."

They approach the boundary of the Broken Brand and the laughter comes to an end. Large equipment lines one side of the property. There are trucks, excavators, and bulldozers. The ground is marked with a series of footprints and tire tracks. But for now, all is quiet. Only the machines remain.

"I guess construction is about to begin," Eli says.

"Yeah, and I'm guessing this is a bad idea," Freddy adds.

The sprawling "Future Home of Foggy Creek Estates" sign towers over the old "No Trespassing" sign. The old sign looks smaller, more faded. It seems to lean to the right just a little more than usual.

"No," Eli decides for them, "this might be our last chance." He quickly devises a plan. "We'll find a couple of sticks," he begins. "Then we'll use the sticks to check the ground ahead of us as we walk. We'll make sure it's stable. Sound good?"

Freddy swallows hard. The moment is suddenly heavy. "Yeah, okay," he says.

They step past the "No Trespassing" sign and Eli says, "Make sure it's a sturdy stick. We might want to poke around a little. See if we find anything shiny." He raises his eyebrows, hoping to remind Freddy that there's a treasure hunt involved in this walk.

They move toward two oak trees that stand alone, towering over the grassy field. Eli finds a suitable stick on the ground, and Freddy jumps to break a small, low-hanging limb from a tree.

They begin to move side by side, poking at the ground before them, eyes on the dirt. Freddy is quiet, so Eli recedes into his own world as well. With each step, he tries to imagine the other feet that have trod this ground over the centuries. He wonders how the terrain has changed over time and how it will soon be completely transformed.

But his thoughts are interrupted by something he sees. "Freddy, look at this," he says. He moves toward a glimmering object between tall blades of grass. It's rounded but thicker and larger than his coin.

Freddy's shadow closes in. He's using the stick like an exaggerated cane, jabbing the ground two feet ahead of him and then allowing his feet to catch up. "What is it?" he asks.

Eli bends down. He lays his books at his side and carefully scrapes at the dirt surrounding the shiny object until he can pull it loose. His heart pounds so loudly that he's sure Freddy can hear it.

Eli holds the object in the palm of his trembling hand. The chain is missing, but without a doubt, it is the gold pocket watch inscribed with the letter W. The very same watch held by the young man in his dream.

As he walks home, Eli's thoughts are consumed
with the pocket watch that is now in his
possession. There is no gold chain attached
like there was in his dream, and he can't prove
to anyone that it once belonged to the nameless
young man who sat alone on a train. But the
W inscription is all the proof Eli needs. It's
definitely the same watch.

Eli reaches his house. In familiar
surroundings, he begins to think rationally.
Maybe he actually saw the pocket watch the
last time he was on the Broken Brand property.

Maybe his eyes saw it, and his brain recorded the image.

Maybe it was during the time when Freddy was sinking into the mud. *That's it*, Eli tells himself. *I was startled. I was desperate. I was scared. Memory can do funny things when mixed with emotion.*

Calmer now, he concludes that the image of the pocket watch was lodged in his subconscious mind. *It bubbled up during a dream. A crazy dream.* He laughs at himself.

Eli deposits his books on the kitchen table. He realizes he's thirsty and gets a glass of water. Then he notices his t-shirt is drenched with sweat.

He goes to his room and puts the glass of water on his desk. He changes to a fresh shirt and throws the sweaty shirt on the floor. Then Eli pulls the pocket watch from the pocket of his jeans.

Suddenly, in his mind, there are flashes like memories. The young man sitting alone. The newspaper. The pocket watch. The fear in his icy blue eyes. The train whistle. *And what about that train whistle? He was awake, wasn't he?*

Eli is less calm now, but he tries to remain rational. He puts the pocket watch on his desk next to the water. *Maybe it wouldn't hurt to do a little online searching*, Eli thinks. *Just for fun. After all, cold, hard facts are always the antidote to fear and mystery.*

He opens his laptop and pauses momentarily, wondering how to begin. The gold coin was minted in 1890. He decides on three terms and types them into the search bar of his browser: train 1890 Foggy Creek.

Immediately, history opens itself to him by way of links. He selects the first one, *Foggy Creek Train Robbery of 1890*, and he begins to read.

The Foggy Creek Heist took place on May 1, 1890. The East-West Railway line kept to its regular schedule, stopping at a station just north of Foggy Creek, Texas, before continuing west.

The East-West Railway was a freight

operation, mainly used for transporting cargo. There was only one passenger car, lined with tall compartments that afforded passengers privacy during their travels. At the time of the robbery, twelve ticketed passengers were aboard.

One of the passengers who boarded the train that day was Winston Steadford, an official of the S & E Bank. Steadford had boarded the train in Abilene. He was tasked with transporting two bags of gold coins to a bank in Lamesa.

Outlaw Carson Wainwright was also a ticketed passenger aboard the train that day. Records indicate he boarded in Fort Worth. When interviewed, passengers could not recall seeing him prior to the heist.

Wainwright was arrested and charged soon after the robbery. Multiple passengers were able to identify him as the robber, mainly by his sandy hair and "icy blue eyes." Each passenger mentioned the eyes as a defining feature. The most convincing testimony was that of banker Winston Steadford.

According to passenger accounts, Wainwright wore a cloth covering most of his face. He carried a large sack and demanded valuables from individuals. Steadford resisted but quickly backed down when Wainwright revealed what looked to be a hand grenade.

Before jumping from the moving train, Wainwright deployed what turned out to be a smoke bomb. There was a loud sound, and the passenger car filled with smoke. Once the smoke cleared, Wainwright had disappeared, along with two bags of gold coins and multiple personal items and petty cash.

Soon after the heist, Wainwright was found at the bottom of a hill just west of Foggy Creek. His leg was injured, which authorities attributed to his jumping from a moving train.

Wainwright was arrested and tried for the crime, but the stolen valuables were never recovered. During his arrest and trial, Wainwright maintained his innocence but offered no explanation as to passenger accounts clearly identifying him as the robber.

By all accounts, Wainwright acted alone. However, because the valuables were never located, some believe Wainwright may have been double-crossed by an accomplice. The location of the valuables taken during the Foggy Creek Heist of 1890 remains one of history's mysteries.

Eli sits back in his chair. He takes a deep breath and looks at the gold coin and pocket watch. *Could the W stand for Wainwright? Did this pocket watch really belong to the train robber? And the biggest question of all, how did this pocket watch enter his mind as he slept?*

He begins another online search, this time for Carson Wainwright. After an image appears at the top of an article, Eli's heart pounds. The image is black and white and a little fuzzy, but it's him. The young man who traveled alone. The young man who robbed everyone in the East-West passenger car in 1890. The young man in Eli's dream. Taking shallow breaths, Eli begins to read.

Carson Wainwright was positively identified by multiple passengers as the masked bandit who robbed passengers aboard the East-West Railway passenger car on May 1, 1890. "It was the eyes," Mrs. Eloise Bertram reported. "Those cold, blue eyes. I will never forget them."

And again, Eli reads that Carson Wainwright maintained his innocence. However, he offered no explanation in his own defense. And the valuables were never recovered.

Eli continues to read and discovers the rest of the young man's story.

After being found guilty by a jury of his peers, Carson Wainwright was sentenced to fifteen years in prison. However, Wainwright did not live to complete his sentence. Within his first year of incarceration, he contracted tuberculosis and died.

Eli scrolls back to the picture. He stares into the outlaw's eyes. He can't see the blue in this black and white photo, but he expects to see a cold, criminal stare. Something hard and rebellious. Instead, he sees only fear. It's the same fear he saw in those eyes the night he first dreamed about the train. The night he first saw the face of Carson Wainwright.

Trembling now, Eli decides to do some more digging. *There must be more to this story*, he thinks. However, the trembling is too much to bear. It feels like the very floor beneath him is shaking.

Eli takes a deep breath and reaches for his water glass. Before he even touches it, the glass overturns. Water spills on the desk. Eli picks up the pocket watch and rushes to push his laptop aside. He grabs his t-shirt from the floor and tries desperately to absorb the water.

Then the lamp flickers. The computer reboots. Suddenly, Eli hears footsteps running toward his room. It's his dad. Knowing he won't be able to explain the pocket watch, Eli quickly slides it into his desk drawer.

He turns to find his dad is in the doorway. There is panic on his face. "Take cover!" he yells. And as he dives beneath the desk with Eli, he adds, "Earthquake!"

After huddling silently beneath his desk for fifteen minutes, Eli's dad speaks. "You okay?" He releases Eli from his tight grip and breathing becomes easier for both of them.

"I'm good," Eli responds. "You good?"

"Yeah," his dad says, crawling out from under the desk. "My knees aren't as young as they used to be, and I whacked my head on the bottom of that drawer, but . . ." He smiles and stands. He reaches out a hand to pull Eli up from the floor. "That was wild. Glad I made it home before it started."

They walk to the kitchen and step around broken glass. They carefully sweep up the glass, and Eli volunteers to heat up a frozen pizza while his dad returns objects to their upright position.

They sit together on the sofa and eat their pizza in front of the local news, like usual. Except everything is most unusual. It's all-hands-on-deck at the news station. They cut to reporters in the field all over town.

A woman who works at the diner is crying and crossing herself. She tells the reporter about the tremors and the screams and the falling items. In the background, people move about with brooms and buckets and bags.

A reporter is on the scene at the grocery store, where two front windows have shattered. Sheriff's deputies stand guard as workers nail plywood to the storefront behind them. The microphone finds a cashier who describes the tremors, the tumbling displays, and the shattering glass.

Eventually, they are back in the studio, speaking remotely to a seismologist, an earthquake expert at a nearby university. He has been tracking seismic activity in the region. The frequency has grown over the past 50 years. He predicts it will continue to grow. Oil drilling from the previous century has destabilized the ground.

Eli relaxes a little. Someone has done the research for him. They've provided the cold, hard facts. This is not a mystery. This is science. But then his heart begins to beat a little faster. The news cuts away from the station to a reporter in the field. They're at the old Broken Brand.

She stands along the roadside. In the background, the towering "Future Home of Foggy Creek Estates" sign still looms large. Beneath it, the faded "No Trespassing" sign now leans at a 45-degree angle.

The reporter stands with developer Kit Landau. He lifts the brim of his bright red Landau Development baseball cap and wipes sweat from his forehead. He explains that a sinkhole has opened on the site. It has swallowed up equipment that was parked along one side of the property. The camera pans across the landscape. No trucks, excavators, or bulldozers remain.

Before they cut back to the station, there is an aerial view of the property that comes from a drone. A large hole punctures the field. Eli can't be certain, but it looks like the same area where Freddy dropped beneath the surface.

"You look a little pale," his dad says. "Are you okay? Wanna talk about it?"

"Oh, yeah, sorry." Eli struggles for words. "It's just all a little shocking, I guess."

His father goes on to describe the science behind earthquakes and sinkholes. He discusses the years of drilling for oil and the way it made the ground unstable. He reassures Eli that they live on solid ground and they will be okay. That they are okay.

Eli listens and nods. He breathes deeply and works to shake away the shadow of superstition. He wonders what Freddy would say right now. Actually, he's pretty sure he knows what Freddy would say. *Score another point for the wrath of angry spirits.*

Over the next few hours, Eli begins to feel calmer, steadier. There have been no more tremors. The house is back to normal. His homework is finished, and he's ready for sleep. He's ready to escape the thoughts and events and fears of the day. However, sleep is once again filled with dreams.

Like last time, there is a train. He's looking through a window once more. But this time, he's on the other side of the train. And this time, he sees Carson Wainwright pressed against a door, hiding. He wears a long black coat over his clothes. Eli notices something he hadn't seen before.

There is a sickle-shaped scar on the left side of the outlaw's face. It's the side that was hidden from Eli the last time. But then the outlaw pulls a bandana from his pocket. He covers his face, and only his eyes remain between the brim of his hat and the bandana. His icy, blue eyes.

Suddenly, he jumps into the aisle of the train. Eli looks for the smoke bomb. He finds it nestled in Wainwright's left hand. True to

Eli's research, it looks like a Civil War-era grenade. Wainwright's right hand holds a sack.

Eli hears a few women scream. He cannot see their faces behind the tall passenger compartments, but he sees their hands as they drop jewelry into the bag. Men empty their wallets. And then a hand reaches out and drops a pocket watch into the bag. It happens quickly, but Eli's almost certain there is a W on the watch.

There isn't time to focus on this now, though. Through the window, Eli sees a passenger stand and confront the outlaw. The man wears a black suit, white shirt, and tall, black hat. Eli instantly recognizes him as Winston Steadford, the banker with the two bags of gold.

The outlaw easily knocks the man aside and holds the grenade aloft. There is silence. Wainwright struggles to lift two bags from the man's seat, but then he moves with surprising speed. Just before making his exit, he pulls the pin and smoke fills the passenger car.

But *wait. Someone moves. Does a passenger try to follow?* Eli is desperate to know, but the smoke is thick, and suddenly the dream ends. Eli awakens out of breath. Sweat drips down his neck. His heart pounds forcefully. In the distance, he hears the long, haunting whine of a train whistle.

Eli settles into his back-row seat in homeroom. Other students gather in clusters, sitting on desks and sharing stories about their earthquake experiences. The stories grow in intensity, each one an effort to top the last.

Mrs. Mendez is nowhere in sight. Eli wonders if she's okay. He wonders if someone should check with the office and report that she's missing. After all, there was an earthquake. He stands, thinking he will be the one to go. But he doesn't get far. He has forgotten that he's now popular and people are interested in him. They want to hear his earthquake story and even his scientific explanation.

Just as he gets to the part about the water spilling, Mrs. Mendez suddenly appears.

Students scatter like ants, reluctantly retreating to their assigned seats. Eli thinks she's going to lose her cool because of all the noise and confusion. But she doesn't. She's beaming. Eli thinks maybe she is nerding out over the earthquake and sinkholes. Exciting stuff for a science teacher.

Mrs. Mendez takes attendance during morning announcements, and Eli can't help but notice that Nolan Bridwell is absent for the second day in a row. No one seems to miss him. Especially Eli.

As soon as the announcements come to an end, Mrs. Mendez seizes the opportunity to share her excitement. "You may notice some TV reporters and cameras on campus today," she tells the class. "Just go about your business and act natural."

This news causes the class to erupt. Now everyone is excited. Mrs. Mendez claps her hands like an elementary school teacher, desperate to regain control.

"I have just completed my interview," she tells them. "And in a moment, the reporters will be speaking with our very own Eli Hancock."

Again, the class erupts. This time, they cheer for Eli. They chant his name. He's a hero. And it feels good.

"With all the news about natural disasters," she continues, yelling to be heard above the chatter, "they want a feel-good story. And Eli's science project going on to the state competition—"

The bell rings and cuts her off. Homeroom ends abruptly, but the cheering and chanting continue. Students huddle around Eli as if they are drawn to him by an invisible force. Hands reach toward him for pats on the back, high fives, and fist bumps. Eli is the man.

He moves with the group, as if floating on a slow-moving river. But as soon as he reaches the door, Mrs. Mendez stops him. She says, "Oh, no sir, you stay here, Eli." She rushes the others out and then explains. "The principal has arranged for my first-period class to meet in the library for a study hall so we can use this room for the interview. The reporter will be here any moment."

As if on cue, a small woman carrying a large microphone enters the room. Her pearly white teeth sparkle in the fluorescent light. She wears a red dress and a thick layer of make-up. Eli recognizes her from the local news. Her name is Cassie Canova. *She looks shorter in person*, he thinks.

The reporter is followed by a cameraman. He's dressed all in black. A knit cap covers his head even though the temperature outside is in the nineties. The camera rests on his shoulder, and he leans his head to one side to make room for it. It's huge.

Cassie Canova introduces herself, and Eli pretends he doesn't know her name. The world doesn't need to find out he's a closet news junkie. He's just risen above nerd status.

Cassie explains that so much of the news right now is about the crazy earthquake and the sinkhole, and it brings the whole community down. The station executives decided they should air a human-interest story, something to lift people's spirits. "And we are all so proud of you, Eli Hancock!" She flashes her hundred-watt smile. "We want to hear all about your science project!"

Suddenly, the camera is rolling. Cassie, the cameraman, the big microphone, the giant camera . . . they are all uncomfortably close to Eli. But he knows he needs to play it cool. So, he does.

Eli shares his hypothesis and his process. He explains the concept of barometric pressure as if he's teaching fourth grade. Cassie repeatedly nods, looking serious. But Eli senses he might be losing her. He decides to tell a joke.

"I was under a lot of *pressure* to get all the data recorded," he says. Cassie picks up on the pun. She laughs a little too loudly. Mrs. Mendez beams in the background. Eli continues to talk about his process of interviewing subjects, getting school records about students' behavior referrals, and aligning his gathered data with barometric pressure readings. But again, he seems to be losing Cassie. Time to wrap it up with another pun.

"So, *whether* or not you believe it, the *weather* can affect your behavior." Eli smiles. He's turning on the charm.

"And cut," Cassie says. "That was perfect!"

As Cassie and the cameraman pack up and leave, Mrs. Mendez issues Eli a pass to his next class. He doesn't even feel the floor beneath his feet as he walks. It's like he's floating. He's finally made it to the top.

Throughout the day, that feeling only intensifies. Eli is a celebrity at Foggy Creek High. People cluster around him at the beginning of every class. Voices shout to him as he walks down the hall. Even seniors know his name. Eli is golden.

After school, he convinces Freddy to walk past the old Broken Brand. "We won't go on the property. I just want to see it!"

Freddy reluctantly concedes. "As long as we

just walk past it. I don't ever want to set foot on that messed-up place again. Those spirits can have it!"

They approach the property and realize it's no longer the desolate wasteland it once was. It looks like ground zero of a natural disaster. A collection of scientists and researchers from the state and nearby universities are setting up equipment.

Eli is fascinated. In his opinion, this day just keeps getting better. Freddy, on the other hand, is freaked out. Everyone wears hard hats, and yellow caution tape outlines the field. All along the tape, over and over again, there is a message repeated in bold, black print. "Danger: Keep Out."

"It was awesome," Eli tells his dad as they carry their plates of spaghetti to the coffee table and cue up the local news. "It's like I'm suddenly a rock star. Just sayin'."

His dad laughs, but then a look of concern casts a small shadow over Eli's triumphant moment. "Just remember that it's called 'fifteen minutes of fame' for a reason. Just sayin'."

The news begins with a reporter on the scene at the old Broken Brand. He reminds the public that this is supposed to be the site of the new Foggy Creek Estates development, with its single-family homes, movie theater, and retail center. But the plan may be in jeopardy.

The camera pulls back to reveal developer Kit Landau standing next to the reporter. "We're confident that this is an isolated event," Landau says. He flashes a reassuring smile and turns to look directly at the camera. "Our engineers and designers are working around the clock. We promised to bring growth to Foggy Creek, and we are going to deliver on that promise."

"Hmm." Eli's dad looks unconvinced. "He talks a good game, but I don't know if he realizes this is beyond his control."

Eli spins spaghetti noodles onto his fork and nods. "I'm guessing he never had a science fair project go to State."

Eli stuffs the tightly wound spaghetti into his mouth. His dad starts to say something, but then he doesn't. He takes a deep breath and returns his attention to the spaghetti and the local news.

There are reporters in more scenes talking to more people about their earthquake experiences. They're basically all the same. They felt a tremor. Something toppled over. They dove for cover. There was a mess to clean up. But they all seem to think they experienced something unique, something no one else can understand.

Finally, it's time for the human-interest story. It's always tucked into the closing sequence. Leave the people with something charming rather than something disturbing.

As he watches, Eli focuses on his hair, his shirt collar, the sound of his voice. Next interview, he'll try to make it sound a little deeper. He makes a few additional mental notes. *Make sure your collar is straight. Maybe let your hair grow out more. Time for a new look.*

He's suddenly pulled from his own mental calculations by his dad's laughter. "You are master of the pun, my son!" He pats Eli on the back. "I'm proud." And then he has to ruin the moment by saying, "Just don't get overconfident, okay?"

Eli takes it like a punch to the gut. His mouth drops open and his eyes squint, narrowing their focus onto the man who just derailed his rise to fame. He wants to say something, but he doesn't know what to say.

Eli picks up his plate. "I'm done," he declares. He carries his plate and water glass to the kitchen. He dumps the rest of his spaghetti in the trash and places his dishes in the dishwasher.

"Eli," his dad pleads. He's standing in the kitchen now, trying to get Eli to stop moving. But Eli refuses to stop. He refuses to look his father in the face.

Eli stands at the refrigerator, refilling his water glass. "I have a lot of homework," he says. "I don't have time for this."

There is a sigh. From the corner of his eye, Eli sees his dad throw his hands in the air. It looks like he rolled his eyes, but Eli can't be sure. He isn't willing to give this man any attention right now.

Eli marches to his room and slams the door. He falls into his chair, and for the next few hours, he tries to focus on homework.

But it's not easy. He's mad. He's hurt. He's offended. He's a whole mix of confused emotions. And the worst thing is, his dad has struck a nerve. There's this part of Eli that is filled with doubt. Maybe he's not as smart as people think. Maybe he's always just one step away from falling into the pit of failure.

There's a knock at his door. "Eli?" His dad isn't giving up.

"I'm studying!" Eli says. Maybe he yells it. He's not sure. He checks the doorknob to be certain that he locked it. He doesn't want to hash this thing out. He wants to be left alone.

"Okay," his dad's voice says. "I'm going to bed. Maybe we can talk in the morning."

Eli doesn't respond. He closes the textbook and looks at his nightstand. The gold coin glows in the dimming light of dusk. Eli smiles. He thinks about luck. Maybe there really is such a thing.

He suddenly remembers sliding the pocket watch into his desk drawer when the earthquake hit. He digs it out and lifts the watch in the palm of his hand. Staring at the W, he thinks, *What's your deal, Carson Wainwright?*

Eli pushes his books aside and opens his laptop. He decides to distract himself with a little more research. Just for a few minutes.

He still has open tabs for sites about Carson Wainwright. But now, by following a couple of links within those sites, Eli stumbles into something new. Or someone, rather. His name is Lance Wainwright. He's the outlaw's long-lost brother. According to the story, he first came to Foggy Creek as next of kin after Carson died in prison. He said he wanted to repair some of the damage his brother had done.

Lance Wainwright seemed to have charmed the locals. He was well dressed and respectable. He was supposedly a businessman from Fort Worth, but the articles provide no information about his line of business. He offered public apologies and donated money to the town coffers. The guy became some kind of local hero.

Eli's eyes widen as he continues to read.

Smitten with the small-town charm of Foggy Creek, Lance Wainwright decided to stay. He purchased 500 acres of land, and with the help of local craftsmen, Wainwright built a large, fashionable home that became the site of some of the finest Foggy Creek social events of the day. The rest of the property was developed into a thriving cattle ranch, which Wainwright named the Broken Brand.

Suddenly, Eli's concentration is shattered by a sound. The house is quiet, and he's fully awake, so this is definitely not a dream. In the distance, Eli hears it approaching. It's the long, low whine of a train whistle. It sounds like it's heading into Foggy Creek from the east.

Eli grabs a jacket and a flashlight. Checking once more to be sure that his bedroom door is locked, he opens the window and climbs out into the darkness. Then he begins to run, determined to put this mystery to rest.

Eli runs faster, and the train whistle grows louder. If he just keeps running, he's sure they will both end up at the same spot. He'll finally see this train, and the phantom whistle can move to the list of cold, hard facts.

He's never run so fast. Eli stops, doubles over, gasps for breath. His glasses are fogged. His heart is a bass drum. The train whistle is deafening at this point. He not only hears the sound. He feels it. It courses through his blood as if the track runs through his body.

Once he's able to breathe more easily, Eli

lifts his head and squares his shoulders. He raises his flashlight and immediately sees the faded "No Trespassing" sign, still leaning at a 45-degree angle. He raises the beam of light and finds the giant "Future Home of Foggy Creek Estates" sign.

Lowering the light, he scans from side to side. Light reflects off the shiny, yellow caution tape. It's stretched out now, and it dangles loosely between stakes. Still, his light reveals the warning printed repeatedly across the plastic ribbon. "Danger: Keep out."

The moon is barely a sliver in the sky, and clouds obscure the starlight. It's dark, and Eli is alone. But he can't let fear stop him now. Allowing the unknown to remain a mystery only encourages fear. It creates uncertainty. It's the stuff myths are made of. It is through science, through facts, and through discovery that we uncover the mystery and make the unknown known. We feed our rational minds instead of feeding the fear. So, he must keep moving forward.

Eli looks beyond the edges of the Broken Brand, trying to reach into the distance. He sees some of the equipment that had been set up by the teams who came to study the area. There are stakes and tiny orange flags. In the distance, ominous gray shadows lurk. They're large and threatening, like the outlines of frozen prehistoric monsters. His flashlight reveals a glimmer of yellow, and soon he realizes he's looking at an excavator and two dump trucks.

But where is the train? The sound persists. It's loud. It still courses through his veins and causes the ground beneath him to vibrate. He hears it. He feels it. But he doesn't see it.

Eli continues to skirt the edges of the property. Finally, though, he ducks beneath the caution tape. He must get closer. It's the only way to find the train before it's gone. He moves carefully, letting the flashlight's beam precede his every step.

Suddenly, in his peripheral vision, Eli senses another light. It's small, bouncing, and moving toward him. Instinctively, he turns off his flashlight, not wanting to be discovered in case he's not alone.

Worst case scenario, he's about to be caught trespassing. No, even worse, he's about to be discovered by a dangerous criminal. Neither scenario is acceptable. So, Eli decides he must abandon this plan tonight. The train whistle seems to be receding. He's probably missed his chance, anyway.

He bends close to the ground, trying to see where he's going without the light to lead him. Moving as quickly as possible, he makes his way back toward the edge of the field. Suddenly, a glimmer of light flashes up from the ground. It's small and slight. But it's enough to stop Eli in his tracks.

He turns the flashlight on but keeps the beam low, aimed directly at the object on the ground. It's gold. It looks like part of a chain. He brushes away dirt and pulls it from its burial place. It's definitely a chain.

For a moment, Eli forgets about the bouncing light that's headed in his direction.

He forgets he's on the Broken Brand, behind the caution tape and the signs. He stares at the chain in his hand, knowing that it was once attached to the pocket watch carried by Carson Wainwright.

Suddenly, he catches a glimpse of light again. It's closer this time. Then a voice comes from somewhere behind the light. "Hey, you there! This is nighttime security. Don't move!"

Eli stands. He grasps the chain tightly and begins to run. He's aware that the security guard is running as well, but Eli has a head start of at least a hundred yards.

Again, his heart pounds like a bass drum. There's a cramp in his side, and his chest burns. But as he draws closer to the yellow caution tape boundary, Eli realizes that his hand burns as well. It's as if he's holding tight to a hot iron. It's scorching his palm, but he refuses to let go.

Eli ducks beneath the caution tape, and suddenly the ground beneath his feet begins to tremble. He's scared, but he doesn't want to let fear paralyze him. He continues to run until the ground shakes so severely that he knows it's another earthquake.

Eli stops. He turns and looks behind him. He shines his light on the guard, who has stopped suddenly as well. And then it happens. The ground opens and the nighttime security guard vanishes.

"No!" Eli screams. He runs back toward the Broken Brand. He doesn't care about the worst-case scenario anymore. He just wants to save this man. But as he reaches the caution tape boundary, he realizes there's nothing he can do.

The ground has opened another deep hole. He watches the "No Trespassing" sign slide into oblivion, swallowed by the Earth. Tears mix with sweat on Eli's face. In a panic, he turns and runs toward home, knowing that if the tremors were felt at his house, his dad would be awake. He'd be banging on Eli's door. Lock or no lock, he would find a way to enter.

As he makes it to his yard, his nerves are on edge. He can't formulate an excuse that sounds plausible. *Why would he be out exploring in the middle of the night? How did this gold watch chain end up in his hand?* He can think of no rational explanation.

But he notices something that begins to calm his nerves and slow the beating of his heart. He realizes that all around him, things are intact. Hanging baskets and potted plants are still in place. Patio chairs and tables adorned with wide umbrellas stand erect in the stillness.

It seems impossible to believe, and yet, all the evidence points to this one conclusion. Somehow, the earthquake did not reach his neighborhood.

Although trembling, Eli manages to hold the chain and flashlight in one hand as he lifts his windowpane with the other. He climbs inside to the safety of his room, and his breathing becomes a little steadier.

His books are stacked on his desk. His lamp is in place on his nightstand. The house is quiet. He's made it.

As his body calms, he becomes increasingly aware of the burning sensation in his palm.

He drops the chain into his nightstand drawer, along with the coin and pocket watch. The three pieces glow with the same eerie light.

Eli quickly closes the drawer and shines the flashlight on his hand. There, across his palm, is a long, red burn mark made by the glowing gold chain.

On the way to school, Eli's dad looks concerned. He drills Eli with questions. "Are you feeling okay? You look kind of pale. Your eyes—"

"I'm fine!" Eli shouts. And then he realizes he shouldn't have shouted. He repeats, quietly this time, "I'm fine."

"Look," his dad says, "I want to apologize for upsetting you so much last night. I was only trying to—"

"Dad, I'm fine. Let's drop it." Eli stares out the window, avoiding eye contact with his dad.

He keeps his fist curled, not wanting to reveal the burn mark.

"So, did you hear about the earthquake?" his dad asks. Obviously, he's trying to change the subject, but for Eli, this topic is a fresh anxiety trigger.

"A new one?" Eli manages, trying to sound unaware.

"Yeah, it was all over the news this morning. Apparently, it was pretty centralized. Probably associated with the new sinkhole."

"A new one?" Again, Eli tries to sound surprised while keeping his face turned toward the window.

"Yeah," his dad continues. "A new sinkhole on the old Broken Brand. The national news picked it up. Foggy Creek is famous."

"Hmm," Eli says. "The ground must be very unstable. Sounds like Foggy Creek Estates might not work out after all."

As the car approaches Foggy Creek High, Eli gathers his things. Before exiting, he stops. He looks straight ahead as he asks, "Did you hear that train last night?"

"A train?" His dad laughs. "Trains haven't run through Foggy Creek for decades. You must've been dreaming."

"Yeah," Eli says, "that's what I figured." And he launches himself into the flurry of high school activity.

Eli's hand burns as he turns the combination on his lock. He opens his locker and tries to concentrate on what he'll need for his first couple of classes. He sees Freddy approaching and nods.

However, Mrs. Mendez cuts in front of Freddy. Her face is stern. Her lips are tight. She stops in front of Eli and crosses her arms. "Eli, you'll need to follow me to the office."

"But homeroom—"

"Will be covered. You and I will be attending a meeting in the office."

Eli shrugs toward Freddy and follows Mrs. Mendez to the office. He figures the reporters might be back. Maybe a follow-up story. But then, why would she look so angry?

They go into a conference room and find a woman wearing a visitor tag. The name scrawled on it in black marker says, "Louise Marshall." Principal Williams enters behind them and closes the door. Everyone wears a serious expression, and Eli's hands begin to sweat. The burn mark stings.

"Eli," Principal Williams begins, "this is Ms. Marshall. She oversees the district science contest, and she's been in close contact with the state association regarding your project. I'm going to hand the meeting over to her, and she can explain."

Eli's mouth is dry. He doesn't understand what's happening. He looks directly at Mrs. Marshall and suddenly wishes he didn't look like someone who stayed up all night. But there's nothing he can do about it now.

"Eli," she begins, "the state association has taken your situation under advisement, and they are withdrawing your project from the competition."

"W-what situation?" Eli's mind empties. He can't seem to form words. He looks from face to face, all of them stern. He feels like he's in trouble. He wants to ask why, but the words won't come.

Mrs. Marshall continues. "Everyone saw the news story, and some questions got raised. Some parents called in. Some people were justifiably upset."

Eli's forehead wrinkles. He manages to croak out a few words. "What kind of questions?"

"Well," Mrs. Marshal says, "some of the data you used seems to be confidential in nature. Behavior reports, for example. How did you access these reports?"

"There's a behavior log in the office," he says. "I picked it up and copied the data I needed."

"And were there names of students attached to that data?"

"Yes," Eli responds. "But those names do not appear in my data."

"However," Principal Williams interjects, "you have no business going through that notebook. It shouldn't have been left out on the counter, but we were having an unusually high number of referrals —"

"Because of the barometric pressure!" Eli says.

Principal Williams is not impressed. He looks irritated and like he's trying to remain calm as he picks up where he left off. "The notebook was left out, and you accessed it without permission."

"I take full responsibility for not asking Eli where he got this data," Mrs. Mendez says.

"No," Principal Williams says. "We all could have done things differently, but the fact remains that Eli is old enough and smart enough to know better. That notebook was property of the office, and it contained confidential information. He had no right to access it."

Mrs. Marshall decides to reclaim the floor. "I'm here to notify you that your project is officially disqualified. Principal Williams will send out an email to parents letting them know there will be consequences for your actions and assuring them the office will keep confidential student behavior records under lock and key from here on out."

"Mrs. Mendez," Eli pleads. "You know I didn't use names."

"And I also know you had no business nosing around in the office behavior log," she says. Her voice is cold, and he realizes this conversation has reached a dead end.

Mrs. Mendez turns away from Eli. "Principal Williams," she says, "I'm sure you have more to discuss with Eli about those consequences Mrs. Marshall referred to. Shall he stay with you?"

"He can return to class while we work out the details," Principal Williams responds. "And then I'll call his father to discuss the disciplinary actions we'll be taking."

The meeting concludes, and Eli exits in a cloud of shame and bewilderment. Students are moving from homeroom to first period. The halls are filled with wall-to-wall people. But there are no high fives. No fist bumps. No shouts of *Way to go, Eli!*

He clutches his books to his chest as

he walks. Eyes dart away from him. People who dare to look at him seem to frown disapprovingly. He sees Freddy and moves in his direction. He raises one hand to make sure Freddy sees him.

That's when someone smacks into him from behind. Eli's books spill across the floor and the crowd scatters back away from them. Then he hears that familiar voice. "Sorry, dweeb! I wasn't watching where I was going!"

Nolan Bridwell passes him and turns back, laughing. This time, it's not just his posse that joins him in laughter. It's everyone. The entire hallway erupts in laughter.

As Nolan walks away, he receives pats on the back, fist bumps, and high fives. Eli hears people saying, *Way to go, Nolan. You're the man.*

Freddy bends and helps Eli retrieve his books. Eli already knows what Freddy is going to say, so he says it for him. "I know. Ignore him."

But Freddy surprises Eli. "I don't know, man. That might be hard to do today."

"Why?"

"Nolan is like some kind of hero," Freddy says. "Suddenly, everybody is saying that he fell out of his chair because of the earthquake." They walk down the hall together.

"But the earthquake hadn't even happened yet," Eli clarifies. They're speaking quickly now. The clock is ticking on the first-period bell.

"I didn't say it made sense," Freddy responds. "I'm just telling you what people are saying. They think Nolan was sensitive to the first rumblings of the Earth. He was a victim. And that makes him a hero."

"Can this day get any worse?" Eli sighs.

"Yeah, dude," Freddy says. "It probably can." Just before breaking away and heading into US history, Freddy adds, "Because from all the talk I'm hearing, while Nolan is a hero, I'm pretty sure you're like the opposite."

The day cannot pass quickly enough.
Everywhere, Nolan is praised and accepted.
Nolan, I'm so glad you're okay! Welcome back! You showed that earthquake who's boss!

Eli can't believe the conversations. He also can't resist the urge to listen. In the hallways and at lunch, he tries to eavesdrop. Without being obvious, of course. He hears Nolan repeat the same story, again and again.

"I felt a little tremor," he lies. "I guess I'm just extra sensitive to that kind of thing." Girls

gush at that line. Eli wants to vomit. The story
continues. "I turned and leaned back to see if
anyone else noticed it. That's when it happened
again, and the chair slid out from under me."

Liar. It's all Eli can think about. Doesn't
anyone remember? It was Eli who was
receiving the attention. Nolan leaned back
and turned around so he could be his usual
insulting self.

But no one seems to remember the truth,
or to even care. Nolan is back on top, so
their world feels right again. They don't ask
questions. They just accept what they want to
believe. What they need to believe so they can
return to their comfort zone.

After school, Eli is on high alert as he
stands in front of his locker, trying to organize
the books he'll need to take home. He knows
that Nolan will pass by any moment and
that he'll be a target for Nolan's sick sense of
humor. And he knows that no one will care.
Well, except maybe Freddy.

"Let's just get out of here," Freddy says.

"It's like you're being slow on purpose. Like you're waiting for him to come around that corner."

"I'm just staying alert," Eli clarifies, although he realizes Freddy may have a point.

Eli rushes to finish. He secures the combination lock and takes one more cautious glance over his shoulder before heading for the exit. When he sees Nolan, he freezes in disbelief.

Nolan walks alongside Mrs. Mendez, but that's not the worst part. They are followed by local reporter Cassie Canova and her cameraman. Cassie is once again in full make-up and carrying a giant microphone. The cameraman is in all black, sporting a knit cap and balancing a mammoth camera on one shoulder. They all file into Mrs. Mendez's classroom, the scene of Nolan's false narrative.

"Look at it this way," Freddy says. "Nolan will be tied up for a while. That gives us a chance to get a head start. Let's go, man."

They begin their walk. They automatically take the regular path that keeps them on sidewalks lined with houses. The path that doesn't lead them near the old Broken Brand.

Freddy is speaking, but Eli isn't really listening. He is distracted. He is plagued by a tremor, but it's not from the Earth. It's from somewhere deep inside him. Only a few days ago, he was on top of the world. He thought his luck had changed. How could it all fall apart so fast?

The boys part ways. Freddy heads off to meet his little sister at her bus stop, and Eli welcomes the solitude of his empty house. It will be at least an hour until his dad gets home. That gives him at least an hour to pull himself together. To crawl out of this hole. To find solid ground.

Eli sinks himself into homework and studying, anything to release his mind from Nolan. He takes breaks to look at the pictures of Carson and Lance Wainwright, still open on his laptop. He wonders if they were twins or if the family DNA was just super strong.

But he doesn't allow himself to become fully immersed in the Wainwright brothers or the Foggy Creek train heist of 1890. If he can't be on the top of the social food chain, he needs to at least make sure his GPA continues to reign.

After a couple of hours of hardcore studying, he takes a break to watch the news with his dad like usual. However, Eli is barely able to eat. He feels ill. His dad expresses concern. When the broadcast reaches the story about local hero Nolan Bridwell, Eli asks to excuse himself.

His dad wants to discuss the science fair fiasco. He says Principal Williams called him and outlined the plan for a series of detentions, which is better than suspension because his grade point average won't be affected. He asks Eli if he wants to talk about it, and Eli declines. End of conversation.

Eli decides to turn in early. He wraps himself in a cocoon of bedcovers and hopes to emerge the next morning as someone new. But he knows it's a vain hope.

Even sleep cannot quiet Eli's mind. In

sleep, dreams come. First, Eli is in a jail cell. He seems to be hovering near the ceiling. He looks down into the cell upon a man. The man is lying on a narrow cot. He's pale, and beads of sweat line his forehead. Eli looks directly into his face. He recognizes the man as Carson Wainwright.

Suddenly, Wainwright coughs. His body convulses, and he holds a rag to his mouth. Eli is sure he sees blood. He looks away. When he looks back again, the coughing has stopped. The prisoner is still. Too still. A chill moves through the air, and Eli realizes that Carson Wainwright is no longer alive.

Next, Eli is at the Broken Brand. He recognizes it from pictures he's seen online. He's in a large house with red velvet lining the stairs and candles lining the walls. A huge chandelier, filled with flames, hangs over the middle of the room.

Guests mill about. There's a lot of laughter. Servers weave through the crowd holding trays aloft. There are finger foods and drinks. There are chocolates and champagne. Over and over again, Eli hears the phrase "Happy New Year." He sees a glittery banner that says 1900.

There is music, but he can't see who's playing it. His vision is limited to one side of the room. There is a man with his back to Eli. He wears a dark suit and shiny boots. People continually enter his orbit. The man pulls a watch from his pocket. On the watch, the letter W is inscribed.

Suddenly, Eli hears someone yell, "Lance!" The man turns. Eli sees his face, his sandy hair, his icy blue eyes. He looks so much like his brother. He looks a little older now, but of course, time has passed. It's the turn of the century.

Another man approaches. Eli can't hear what the man says, but he sees Lance Wainwright toss his head back and laugh. And in that moment, in the glittering candlelight, Eli makes a startling realization. He doesn't need to hear what's said. What he sees tells the whole story.

Suddenly, Eli's thoughts flashback to what he had seen in the jail cell. He remembers the face of Carson Wainwright as he lay dying. The face that was pale and splotched with sweat. The face that was smooth and unblemished.

However, as Eli looks upon the face of Lance Wainwright, he sees a very distinct sickle-shaped scar nearly glowing on the left side of his face. The same sickle-shaped scar Eli had seen on the face of the bandit.

It's still dark outside when Eli awakens. There is an eerie glow in his room, and he knows where it's coming from. Eli slides the nightstand drawer open carefully.

His Broken Brand relics glow with a new intensity. He slams the drawer shut. He almost laughs to think that he once entertained the idea that the coin brought him luck. As if he were the kind of person to believe in luck. He believes in science and facts.

Then he thinks about Freddy and the angry spirits. Maybe Freddy and his mom are onto something. Lance Wainwright robbed the train and allowed his brother to take the fall. To call Carson Wainwright an angry spirit seems justifiable. If you believe in such things.

Eli remembers the fear in Carson's face as he sat on the train. He also remembers someone moving in the smoke. They were following the robber, perhaps trying to stop him. It had to be Carson. *But when he was arrested, why didn't he say something? Why didn't he defend himself? Why would he claim his innocence but not tell them about his brother?*

Eli sits up with resolve. He can't continue asking questions. If he does, he will continue to get answers in his dreams. He will continue to find relics of the past. And these relics don't bring good luck. If anything, they are a curse.

If he ever wants to be free of this curse, Eli knows what he must do. He dresses for school. He carefully deposits the coin, the pocket watch, and the gold chain in his backpack.

Eli hears his dad shuffling around in the kitchen. Ready, Eli grabs his backpack and stack of books, and he heads to the pantry for a protein bar. His dad stands at the kitchen window, coffee mug in hand, and yawns. Outside, an orange glow pierces the darkness, and soft light begins to spill across the sky.

"Hey Dad," Eli says, "I forgot to tell you. I have to go in early for a science club thing. I'm just going to walk."

His dad is startled into consciousness. "Eli, we never got a chance to talk last night. Give me five minutes," he says, "and I can drive you."

"Thanks, but I'd really rather walk," Eli tells him. "It'll give me a chance to appreciate that sunrise."

They both pause before the window, their gazes reaching toward dawn. Eli's dad breaks the silence and says, "Well, if you're sure—"

"I'm sure," Eli replies. He turns and leaves.

Eli walks purposefully, but he doesn't take a direct path to school. That was never his intention. Instead, he heads for the Broken Brand. By the time he reaches it, the sun has crawled higher, and hazy morning light has overtaken the darkness.

A thick cloud of fog hovers over the ground. The caution tape is barely visible through the gray mist. But Eli knows exactly where he is. And he knows exactly what he must do.

He lays his stack of books carefully on the ground at his side. He slides his backpack off and drops it in front of him. He kneels and pulls the zipper, then hastily looks around to be sure no one is watching. The cover of fog reassures him, and he continues.

He reaches past his notebooks, his lunch, his calculator, and the other tools of his rational life. He has to dig. The items he's searching for have settled at the bottom of the bag. And yet, they still glow. They still call to him.

Now he holds them in his left hand. He stands and takes a deep breath. These relics have a story to tell, but Eli no longer desires to be the bearer of this dark history. One by one, he hurls each relic over the yellow caution tape, into the mist, onto the living, breathing patch of earth that was once owned by outlaw Lance Wainwright.

Suddenly, the fog begins to swirl. Dark clouds move briskly across the sky overhead, obscuring the morning sun. The ground begins to tremble, and Eli loses his balance.

Heart pounding, Eli scrambles onto his hands and knees. He gathers his books and his backpack. He adjusts his glasses and he runs. As fast as his legs will carry him, he runs.

The farther he gets from the Broken Brand, the more stable the ground becomes. The mist clears, clouds part, and sunlight spills across his path. Eli breathes deeply. For the first time in days, he feels free.

After a wonderfully uneventful day at school, Eli sits by his dad's side on the sofa, embracing the dull security of this routine. They dig into a spectacularly ordinary noodle casserole and prepare for the evening news.

"Did you hear there was another earthquake at the old Broken Brand?" his dad asks.

"A new one?" Eli responds. He pretends to be totally unaware, and he knows he's pulling it off.

"Yeah, another small one. It was pretty

localized. But still, there's no way that land is stable enough for Foggy Creek Estates." His dad raises a forkful of noodle casserole, and just before depositing it into his mouth, he adds, "I hope that developer has a Plan B."

Eli nods. "You always have to have a Plan B."

The news begins with a discussion of the tremor, but the tremor is not the highlight. Instead, there is breaking news at the site of the old Broken Brand, and reporter Cassie Canova is on the scene.

Eli pictures the large microphone, the bright smile, and the guy dressed in black with his giant camera. He remembers the awkward feeling of them moving into his personal space, and he's glad he's not the guy in front of the camera this time.

Instead, the guy in front of the camera is developer Kit Landau. And he's not looking disappointed. In fact, he's smiling. Big time. His artificially white teeth practically glow.

Apparently, there has been a big discovery and it's something exciting. Kit Landau reports that archeologists have been called in. The historical society has been alerted. "Who knows what this will lead to?" Kit Landau asks.

Then he raises a gloved hand, and the camera zeroes in on the object he holds. It's a gold coin. Etched on the front, a woman's head is adorned with a crown that says "Liberty." Around her head, stars line the coin, and beneath her, the year 1890 glimmers in the camera's light.

Eli rubs his eyes, disbelieving. "But what . . . how . . ." He struggles for words that won't form.

"Yeah, I know," his dad responds. "I mean, it's in good condition and worth a lot, but it's not—"

He stops because Kit is talking again. "I knew it was a good omen," he says. "So I scouted around a little more. Being careful, of course. I kept my distance from the sinkholes. And then I found this."

He holds up a pocket watch. It's round and gold and inscribed with the letter W. "It was just sitting there in the soil, looking up at me," Kit Landau says. "Like it was begging to be found."

The camera cuts to Cassie Canova. Her eyes are wide and her tone is overly enthusiastic. She asks Landau, "In light of this startling turn of events, have you changed your plans for the old Broken Brand property?"

With increasing excitement, he says, "We have to be careful because the ground has proven itself to be a little unstable." He laughs, as if that's some kind of joke. "But we want to bring in crews to do some excavating. A professor over at the university thinks a lost treasure could be buried on this property."

"A lost treasure?" Cassie asks. Then she continues with a question that's an obvious set-up. "Could it be the missing valuables from the 1890 Foggy Creek train heist?"

"That's exactly what we're hoping, Cassie." Kit contorts his face into a serious expression. Or maybe he's going for a studious look. "Back in 1890, outlaw Carson Wainwright rode aboard the passenger car of an East-West Railway train. He stole valuables from individuals aboard the train, and he made off with two bags of gold coins being transported by a banker."

Landau pauses before continuing. He raises his eyebrows. It's an obvious move to create tension and build drama. "Oddly enough," he says, "this property was owned by Lance Wainwright, a successful cattle rancher who just happened to be the brother of outlaw Carson Wainwright."

"It sounds like you know your history," Cassie gushes. Kit Landau is eating this up.

"Yeah, I am a bit of a history buff," he says. He grins at the camera. "And I believe in destiny. While this discovery changes my plans for the property, I don't consider it a setback. I consider it a stroke of good luck. We're uncovering treasure and unlocking a mystery. You know, this story could make good a book. Or maybe a movie."

Landau turns toward the reporter and says, "Cassie, I can't wait to see what happens next!"

Eli listens to the words coming from Landau's mouth, but he's not focused on

Landau's face. He's focused on the objects in the developer's hands. Eli leans forward and adjusts his glasses. The coin. The watch. He swears he can see them glow.

And that's not all. In the distance, Eli hears something. And by the startled look on Kit Landau's face and the way he shuffles nervously and diverts his eyes, it's obvious that Landau hears it too. The long, haunting whine of a train whistle.

ABOUT THE AUTHOR

Susan Koehler LOVES books! She loves to read them, and she loves to write them. Susan is the author of five nonfiction books for children, and two novels for young readers. She has also written several professional resource books for teachers. As a veteran educator, Susan loves to work with students and teachers. You can learn more about Susan's books, author visits, and writing workshops at susankoehlerwrites.com.